Dear Parent:

Congratulations! Your child is taking the first steps on an exciting journey. The destination? Independent reading!

STEP INTO READING® will help your child get there. The program offers books at five levels that accompany children from their first attempts at reading to reading success. Each step includes fun stories, fiction and nonfiction, and colorful art. There are also Step into Reading Sticker Books, Step into Reading Math Readers, and Step into Reading Phonics Readers— a complete literacy program with something to interest every child.

Learning to Read, Step by Step!

Ready to Read   Preschool–Kindergarten
• big type and easy words • rhyme and rhythm • picture clues
For children who know the alphabet and are eager to begin reading.

Reading with Help   Preschool–Grade 1
• basic vocabulary • short sentences • simple stories
For children who recognize familiar words and sound out new words with help.

Reading on Your Own   Grades 1–3
• engaging characters • easy-to-follow plots • popular topics
For children who are ready to read on their own.

Reading Paragraphs   Grades 2–3
• challenging vocabulary • short paragraphs • exciting stories
For newly independent readers who read simple sentences with confidence.

Ready for Chapters   Grades 2–4
• chapters • longer paragraphs • full-color art
For children who want to take the plunge into chapter books but still like colorful pictures.

STEP INTO READING® is designed to give every child a successful reading experience. The grade levels are only guides. Children can progress through the steps at their own speed, developing confidence in their reading, no matter what their grade.

Remember, a lifetime love of reading starts with a single step!

For Mom and Dad
—L.H.

For Mami and Beel. Much love and thanks for your constant support . . . y comidas calientes!
Las quiero mucho.
—V.D.

Special thanks to MaryJoy Martin for sharing J. Dawson Hidgepath's story. Her vivid account, "The Determined Lover," appears in her book Twilight Dwellers: Ghosts, Ghouls, and Goblins of Colorado *(Pruett Publishing, 1985). Thanks also to the Hill-Carter family and to Jordanna Musard and Christine Crumlish Joyce of Shirley Plantation for information about Martha Hill Pratt; and to Kerry Livingston of the Stinson Beach Library and Len Chapman, current resident of Easkoot House, for help with the captain's tale. Two books were particularly useful in researching the legend of the mooncusser: Elizabeth Reynard's* The Narrow Land *(Houghton Mifflin Co., 1934) and Patricia Edwards Clyne's* Ghostly Animals of America *(Dodd, Mead & Co., 1977).*

Photo credits: p. 18 courtesy of the U.S. Coast Guard Historian's Office; pp. 21 and 28 courtesy of Shirley Plantation, Charles City, Virginia; p. 33 copyright © Sara Wendel; and pp. 40 and 48 courtesy of Len Chapman.

www.stepintoreading.com

Educators and librarians, for a variety of teaching tools, visit us at
www.randomhouse.com/teachers

Library of Congress Cataloging-in-Publication Data
Haskins, Lori.
Spooky America : four real ghost stories / by Lori Haskins ; illustrated by Viviana Diaz.
    p. cm. — (Step into reading. A step 4 book)
SUMMARY: Recounts four fact-based tales of hauntings, including a ghost horse on the coast of Massachusetts, a haunted painting at a Virginia plantation, a skeleton in Colorado, and a ghostly sea captain of California.
ISBN 0-375-82500-2 (trade) — ISBN 0-375-92500-7 (lib. bdg.)
1. Ghosts—United States—Juvenile literature. [1. Ghosts.]
I. Diaz, Viviana, ill. II. Title. III. Series: Step into reading. Step 4 book.
BF1472.U6H376 2003   133.1'0973—dc21   2002153073

Printed in the United States of America First Edition 10 9 8 7 6 5 4 3 2 1

STEP INTO READING, RANDOM HOUSE, and the Random House colophon are registered trademarks of Random House, Inc.

STEP INTO READING®

STEP 4

SPOOKY AMERICA

FOUR REAL GHOST STORIES

BY LORI HASKINS

ILLUSTRATED BY VIVIANA DIAZ

Random House 🏠 New York

Is America haunted?

Across the country, in tiny towns and in big cities, you hear ghost stories. Thousands of them! Ask around. Chances are, there's a strange and spooky tale about your hometown.

But are these stories true?

Many of them, like the ones in this book, started with real people, places, or events. Somewhere along the way, legend got mixed up with history. Today it's hard to tell what *really* happened.

What we do know is that at one time or another, people believed the four stories you're about to read.

The question is . . . do you?

1
THE MOONCUSSER'S HORSE

Monomoy Point
Cape Cod, Massachusetts
September 1660

The old pirate peers into the sky.

"Perfect," he whispers. He cackles to himself.

Not a star is shining. A thin sliver of moon is hidden behind dark clouds. It's a pitch-black night.

A perfect night for a shipwreck.

Over three hundred years ago, ships sank along Cape Cod almost every week. Sailors called it the Graveyard of the Atlantic.

There were many reasons for the shipwrecks. Thick fog. Strong currents. Fierce storms.

There was another, more terrible reason, too. Mooncussers.

Mooncussers were pirates. But not the usual kind. They didn't sail the ocean, looking for ships to attack. Instead, mooncussers worked on land. They paced the shore in the dead of night. Over their heads they swung lanterns.

8

Off in the distance, a ship would see the lanterns bobbing. The captain would mistake them for the lights of another ship, safely passing Cape Cod. He'd follow the lights—and crash onto the shore!

As soon as the ship wrecked, the mooncussers sprang into action. They murdered the crew and stole the cargo.

The pirates' trick worked only on the darkest of nights, when the moonlight wouldn't give them away. That's how they got their name. On bright nights, they "cussed" the moon!

One pirate, the Monomoy Mooncusser, was especially greedy. He didn't want to share his loot. So he worked alone, on an empty spit of land called Monomoy Point.

His only partner was a beautiful horse.
He chose her for her color. Except for a
small white patch on her forehead, she was
all black.

In the dark, she was almost invisible.

11

One moonless night, the pirate went to work. He tied a lantern to his horse's mane, and another to her tail. He lit the wicks inside. Yanking on the horse's reins, he trotted her along the shore.

Above, thick storm clouds rolled in. Rain began to fall, first lightly and then in great sheets. The wind shrieked.

The pirate grinned. The more awful the weather, the more likely a ship would wreck!

The waves beat higher and higher against the sand. The horse whinnied nervously. But the pirate ignored her.

He ignored the waves, too. Even when they soaked his ankles. Then his knees. Then his hips.

Suddenly, a huge wall of water rose up. It crashed over the shore—and swept the pirate and his horse out to sea!

The mooncusser screamed for his horse to take him on her back.

But the horse broke free. She swam away, hard and fast through the churning water. First the lantern on her mane sputtered and went out. Then the one on her tail went black, too.

That's when the pirate knew he was doomed. It would be impossible to spot his horse in the darkness. After all, that is why he chose her.

At dawn, the mooncusser's body washed up on the shore.

His horse was nowhere to be found.

A month passed. The moon grew full, then shrank to a sliver again.

Sailors began to report a strange sight. A horse was swimming around Monomoy Point in the middle of the night. Except for a black patch on her forehead, she was all white. A gleaming, ghostly white!

It was the mooncusser's horse. Now that she was free from the pirate, she no longer wrecked ships. She rescued them instead!

For the next hundred years, sailors followed the bright white horse to safety.

Today, ships have little trouble sailing around Cape Cod. There is rarely a shipwreck anymore.

But some sailors swear that on the darkest of nights, you can still see the mooncusser's horse. They say she has never stopped trying to make up for the mooncussing at Monomoy Point.

And she never will.

Today the ghost horse isn't the only help that sailors have.
A lighthouse was built on Monomoy Point in 1823.

2
PICKY AUNT PRATT

Shirley Plantation
Charles City, Virginia
January 2002

A visitor stares at a painting on the first floor of the Shirley Plantation museum.

The painting hangs a bit crooked. Otherwise, it looks perfectly ordinary.

The woman in the picture is Martha Hill Pratt. Her brother-in-law built this grand house nearly three centuries ago. Members of her family still own it today. They call Martha "Aunt Pratt."

And they know her painting is not ordinary at all!

Aunt Pratt was born at Shirley. She lived there until she married and moved to England in the early 1700s.

After she left, her picture was hung in the bedroom on the first floor. It was a nice, sunny spot. Across the room was a big window. Outside lay the green grass of the family cemetery.

*Shirley Plantation. Some people believe
Martha Hill Pratt's spirit haunts the house.*

The painting stayed in the same
place for the next hundred years or so.
Generations of the family came and went.

Finally, in the 1800s, the family decided
to change things around. They took down
Aunt Pratt's picture and put it in the attic.
That's when the trouble started!

Around midnight, the family heard a sound. It was coming from upstairs.

Tap, tap, tap.

The family checked the attic. Everything seemed fine. But the spooky noise didn't stop. Night after night, it continued.

Tap, tap, tap.

The family was baffled. The only thing different was Aunt Pratt's painting. Could the picture have something to do with the tapping? It seemed impossible.

They moved the picture to the third floor.

The noise moved, too!

Tap, tap, tap.

They tried the second floor.

Tap, tap, tap.

Finally, they hung the painting on the first floor again.

That night, the house was silent!

Aunt Pratt was trying to tell them something. She wanted her old spot back! Maybe it was because she could see out the window. She could watch over her loved ones in the cemetery outside.

The family gave in to Aunt Pratt's wishes. They left the painting on the first floor. There it stayed for at least another hundred years.

Then, in 1974, Aunt Pratt's picture was moved again—this time all the way to New York City! There was a display of haunted objects at Rockefeller Center. Aunt Pratt's picture was going to be part of it.

No one knew it would be the main attraction!

The minute the painting was hung, it began to act up. It rattled against the wall.

Tap, tap, tap.

Then it started to swing on its hook! Back and forth, higher and higher. Aunt Pratt's picture would not stay still!

Crowds gathered to see the restless painting. NBC News even ran a report about it! The people at Rockefeller Center locked the painting in a closet overnight for safekeeping.

Aunt Pratt didn't like that at all!

The night watchman heard loud banging coming from the closet. He was pretty sure he heard a woman crying, too.

The closet door was opened. There lay the picture, facedown on the floor. Its frame was smashed!

Aunt Pratt's family decided she had had enough. Once the frame was fixed, they took the picture home. They hung it in its favorite place—for good.

These days, Aunt Pratt seems happy. There's just one thing. In 2001, the first floor needed repairs. Jordanna Musard works at Shirley. She took the picture down until the repairs were done.

Now whenever Jordanna goes into the museum, the painting hangs crooked!

It's just a friendly reminder from Aunt Pratt . . . *leave me alone!*

Martha Hill Pratt's mysterious picture.

3
THE BONY BACHELOR

Buckskin Joe Mining Camp
Buckskin Joe, Colorado
March 1866

J. Dawson Hidgepath is dead.

Annie Lewis is sure of it. She saw him buried last year with her own two eyes. Yet here he is, standing on her front porch!

He's got his same old brown hat on his head. That is, on the skull that *used* to be his head.

"I think I'm going to faint," Annie whispers.

The skeleton pulls off his hat. He drops to one bony knee.

"Annie," J. Dawson says softly. "Will you marry me?"

Flump! Down goes Annie.

In the 1860s, most men went to Colorado looking for one thing. Gold.

J. Dawson Hidgepath went looking for two things. Gold . . . and a bride.

The lonely miner arrived in 1863. That year, he asked nearly every woman in town to be his wife. The problem was, most of them were already married!

That didn't stop J. Dawson. Time after time, he knelt with his dusty brown hat in his hand. "Will you marry me?"

The women's husbands weren't pleased. Some of them threatened J. Dawson with fists. Some threatened him with shotguns!

You might think that's how J. Dawson met his end. But no.

One hot July day in 1865, J. Dawson couldn't find any ladies to visit. So he decided to go for a hike on nearby Mount Bross. Halfway up the trail, he took a wrong step—and plunged to his death off the side of the mountain!

Buckskin Cemetery, where J. Dawson Hidgepath's bones were said to be buried—and buried, and buried again....

The people of Buckskin Joe buried J. Dawson in the cemetery just outside of town. They thought his courting days were over.

They were dead wrong!

It wasn't long before J. Dawson started showing up again. His skeleton knocked on every door in town. First he called on the town seamstress.

Then the schoolteacher.

Then the barmaid from the saloon.

Each time, the people of Buckskin Joe buried J. Dawson's bones again.

Each time, he came back.

The townspeople dug his grave deeper. They put heavy rocks on it. But nothing kept J. Dawson from looking for love!

He proposed to the barber's daughter. The banker's sister. Even the mayor's wife!

Finally, the people of Buckskin Joe couldn't take it anymore.

They stuffed J. Dawson's bones into a sack. In the middle of the night, they rode over the mountains to the town of Leadville.

There, they stopped at an outhouse. They carried J. Dawson's bones inside— and dumped them down the hole!

That should do it, they figured. Even if he got out, he'd be too embarrassed by his smell to go courting!

The plan worked. From then on, the women of Buckskin Joe were left alone.

Of course, the Leadville ladies had their own troubles. Each time they visited the outhouse, they heard a soft voice from below.

"Will you marry me?"

4
BY HOOK OR BY CROOK

Easkoot House
Stinson Beach, California
July 1903

Old Captain Easkoot is stubborn.

He doesn't care how hot the summer gets. He doesn't want any kids on his beach.

It's not hard to keep them away. After all, the captain looks scary.

His face is rough from years at sea, and he always wears a scowl on it. His left hand is shriveled up like a claw. Every morning he straps a shiny gold hook to his wrist. When anyone comes near, he just shakes the hook and hollers.

"Stay off my land!"

Sure enough, the kids steer clear. They are all terrified of Captain Easkoot.

And he's not even a ghost . . . *yet!*

Captain Easkoot, without his infamous hook.

Alfred Derby Easkoot wasn't always scary. But he *was* always stubborn.

As a boy, he wanted to become a sailor. He ran off to sea when he was just nine years old! Later, his hand was burned in a fire on the ship. But that didn't stop him. He learned to sail one-handed. He even became the captain of his own ship.

Years passed. Alfred's ship went down near Stinson Beach. The stubborn captain decided to stay right there.

He built a fine house on the beach and
married a lady named Amelia Dumas.
Together, they opened a campground.
Alfred told stories and Amelia sang songs
for the campers. Everyone liked the sea
captain and his pretty wife.

Then, one terrible evening, Amelia fell into Alfred's arms—dead! Doctors said her heart had burst.

After that, Alfred's own heart was never the same. He turned angry and bitter. He stopped welcoming people to his beach. Instead, he spent the rest of his life scaring them away.

Captain Easkoot died at two o'clock in the morning on December 10, 1905.

The next day, the hearse came for his body. Four men struggled to carry his coffin across the loose sand. One of the men slipped.

The coffin fell. Captain Easkoot's gold hook tumbled out. Before anyone could pick it up, the waves swept the hook out to sea!

Twenty-five years passed. Captain Easkoot's house sat empty. Vines grew over the windows. The porch sagged.

The kids who had been afraid of the captain grew up. They hardly thought of him anymore.

All that changed one misty night in 1930. A light flickered in an upstairs window at the old Easkoot house.

Someone was in there. Moving from room to room. Searching for something.

The front door creaked open. A figure stumbled down the steps. It looked like a man. He fell to his knees on the beach.

With one hand, he pawed the sand.

"Where's my hook?" he hollered. "GIVE ME MY HOOK!"

The news spread through Stinson Beach. Captain Easkoot was back!

People claim the captain's ghost haunts the beach to this day.

He appears at two o'clock in the morning—the hour of his death. And he spends each night searching for his gold hook.

Will he ever give up? It doesn't seem likely. After all, Captain Easkoot was always stubborn. And he probably always will be!

Easkoot House—a haunted house?